FIFTY EIGHT

A TRUE STORY!
PIG ON THE TITANIC

by Gary Crew

pictures by Bruce Whatley

HARPERCOLLINSPUBLISHERS

Pig on the Titanic: A True Story
Copyright © 2005 by Gary Crew
Illustrations copyright © 2005 by Bruce Whatley
Manufactured in China by South China Printing Company Ltd.
All rights reserved.
www.harperchildrens.com

Library of Congress Cataloging-in-Publication Data
Crew, Gary, date.
   Pig on the Titanic : a true story / by Gary Crew ; pictures by Bruce Whatley.—1st
ed.
      p.   cm.
   Summary: On the disastrous night when the ocean liner *Titanic* sinks, the sounds of a
pig-shaped music box cheer children escaping in a lifeboat.
   ISBN 0-06-052305-0 — ISBN 0-06-052306-9 (lib. bdg.)
   1. Titanic (Steamship)—Juvenile fiction: [1. Titanic (Steamship)—Fiction. 2. Music
box—Fiction. 3. Music—Fiction. 4. Shipwrecks—Fiction.] I. Whatley, Bruce, ill.
II. Title.
PZ7.C867Pi 2005   2003008729
[E]—dc21   CIP
                                                                     AC

Typography by Al Cetta
1 2 3 4 5 6 7 8 9 10
❖
First Edition

A pig on a passenger liner?
Impossible!
No! No! It's me . . . Maxixe, the music box pig!
Let me tell you my story. . . .

WHITE STAR LINE ❖ · AMERICAN LINE

My mistress was Miss Edith Rosenbaum, the famous fashion buyer. Miss Edith was leaving Paris for New York to show her latest designs. She was sailing aboard the *Titanic*, the biggest passenger liner in the world—but since the voyage could be dangerous, her mother bought her a good-luck charm.

Me . . . Maxixe, the musical French pig.

Oui, oui!

Oink, oink!

You wind up my tail and I play the maxixe!

Oooh-la-la!

"There is nothing better than music to chase your troubles away." Miss Edith laughed when she unwrapped me. "Thank you, Mama."

How proud I was to be sailing aboard
such a grand ship.

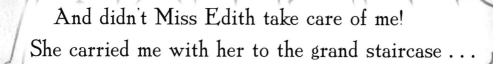

And didn't Miss Edith take care of me!
She carried me with her to the grand staircase . . .

To the reading room . . .

To the captain's table . . .

Everywhere!

Then one cold, dark night the *Titanic* struck an iceberg so big and so terrible that it tore the ship open.

The sea came flooding in.

No one had expected this to happen—not to the biggest passenger liner in the world.

Oh, what a disaster!

But when the sailors told Miss Edith that the *Titanic* was sinking, she did not panic. She remembered me, her good-luck charm.

"Maxixe!" she cried. "Maxixe! I must take you with me when we abandon ship!"

Miss Edith held me close and hurried to the deck. There was so much confusion. The ship was sinking fast, and the deck was slippery and covered with ice.

Everyone was calling for help, especially the children. "Where is my mama?" they cried. "Where is my papa?"

But when a sailor saw that she was not going to get into a lifeboat herself, he shouted, "Madame, if you will not save yourself, I will save your baby!" And snatching me from under her arm, he threw me into a lifeboat!

Me?
A baby?

I landed beneath everybody's feet. There were many bare toes and stockings and shoes and boots.

But my mistress jumped in and picked me up.

Seeing the passengers suffering, my mistress tucked me under her arm and hurried to their aid. "Do not worry about me," she told the sailors. "I have Maxixe to protect me. You must save the other women and children first."

But when a sailor saw that she was not going to get into a lifeboat herself, he shouted, "Madame, if you will not save yourself, I will save your baby!" And snatching me from under her arm, he threw me into a lifeboat!

Me?
A baby?

I landed beneath everybody's feet. There were many bare toes and stockings and shoes and boots.

But my mistress jumped in and picked me up.

Maxixe! Miss Edith cried. "Are you all right? The children, they are so cold and frightened. They need your help. If I wind up your tail, can you still play your song?"

Oui, oui!
It's me, Maxixe.
Of course I can play!

So Miss Edith wound up my tail. Round and round it went.
Round and round. It was very crooked, but I played.

First I saw a little smile. Then I heard a giggle. My song had
made the children laugh!

All night long the boys and girls passed me from hand to hand, winding up my tail and singing along to my music, until at last a rescue ship came by.

"Maxixe, you are so brave," my mistress said as she sat on the safe, dry deck.

"Yes! Yes!" the children cried. "Maxixe, you are a hero!"

Me?

A hero?

No, no. It's impossible! I am only Maxixe . . . the musical pig. I was made to take away your troubles. My music will always do that.

Just listen. . . .

Oui, oui!
Oooh-la-la . . .
Oink, oink!

*Miss Edith Rosenbaum
and Maxixe*

AUTHOR'S NOTE

At 11:40 P.M. on the night of April 14, 1912, the American-owned
White Star liner *Titanic* hit an iceberg off the coast of Newfoundland.
The *Titanic* sank two hours and forty minutes later. Of the 2,228
people aboard, 1,523 lost their lives in the frozen sea; 158 of these were
women and children. The sinking of the *Titanic* is one of the worst maritime
disasters of all time.

While there are always tales of great individual courage in any disaster, the sinking of
the *Titanic* seems to have more than its fair share. There are accounts of passengers giving
up their places in lifeboats so that others could live, of women refusing to leave their
husbands when the ship went down, but perhaps one of the most memorable acts of human
compassion was performed by Edith Rosenbaum—and her wonderful music box pig, Maxixe.

Edith was working as a fashion buyer and was sailing aboard the *Titanic* to show her
new line of French dresses to clients in the United States. But just before she left France
for America, she was involved in a terrible automobile accident and was lucky to escape
with her life. So Edith's mother gave her Maxixe, a little music box pig that played the
maxixe, a dance popular at the time. She hoped its happy song would bring her daughter good
luck on her long voyage aboard the *Titanic*.

Edith would need that good luck—and that happy song.

When the *Titanic* struck the iceberg, Edith refused to enter a lifeboat and did so only
when a sailor, mistaking Maxixe for a baby, threw the music box pig into lifeboat number
11. There were several terrified children in that lifeboat, and seeing their fear, Edith knew
exactly what to do. Although Maxixe was badly damaged in the fall, Edith wound up its tail,
and the musical pig entertained the children with its bright and cheery tune until they were
rescued.

In later life Edith continued to bring her fashions into the United States. She became
very famous and lived a long and happy life. Edith died on April 4, 1975—63 years almost
to the day since that dreadful night when the *Titanic* went down.

As for Maxixe, it is kept in very special glass case in a private collection in New York.
And as far as I know, Maxixe would still play for you, if you were to ask. . . .